This book belongs to

. . . .

For Tana, with love

Published by
MANTRA PUBLISHING LTD
5 Alexandra Grove
London N12 8NU

跟我一樣的嬰兒
A BABY JUST LIKE ME

Susan Winter

Chinese Translation by Sylvia Denham

MANTRA

森在瑪花的家留宿。

Sam was staying the night at Martha's house.

他們談及瑪花的初生妹妹。

They were talking about Martha's new baby sister.

「她明天便會回家。」瑪花說。

"She's coming home tomorrow," said Martha.

「她將會做甚麼？她會不會在我們的樂隊演奏？」森問道。「她會做所有的事情，媽媽說她會跟我一樣。」

"What's she going to do? Will she play in our band?" asked Sam.
"She'll do *everything*. Mum says she's going to be just like me."

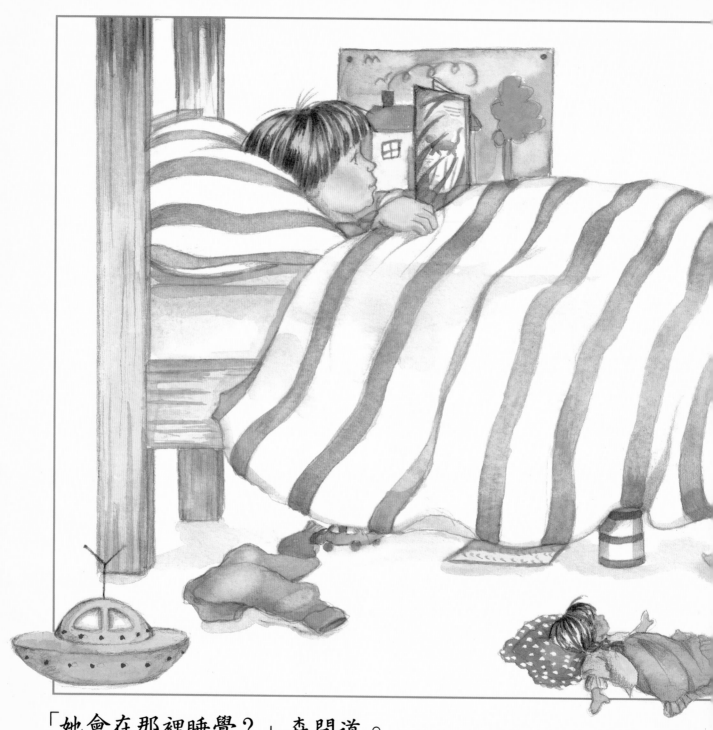

「她會在那裡睡覺？」森問道。

"Where's she going to sleep?" asked Sam.

「就在這個籃裡 ，但我想她會比較喜歡我的下格床。」瑪花說。

"In this basket, but I think she'll like my bottom bunk better," said Martha.

她們爲新生嬰兒將所有東西準備好，如果
她是跟瑪花一樣，她可以穿瑪花的舊衣服，
玩她的舊玩具，甚
至用她的舊便桶。

They got everything ready for the new baby. If she was going to be just like Martha she could wear Martha's old clothes, play with her old toys, and even use her old potty.

當瑪花的媽媽回家時，她抱拿着一大包。

When Martha´s mum came home she was carrying a bundle.

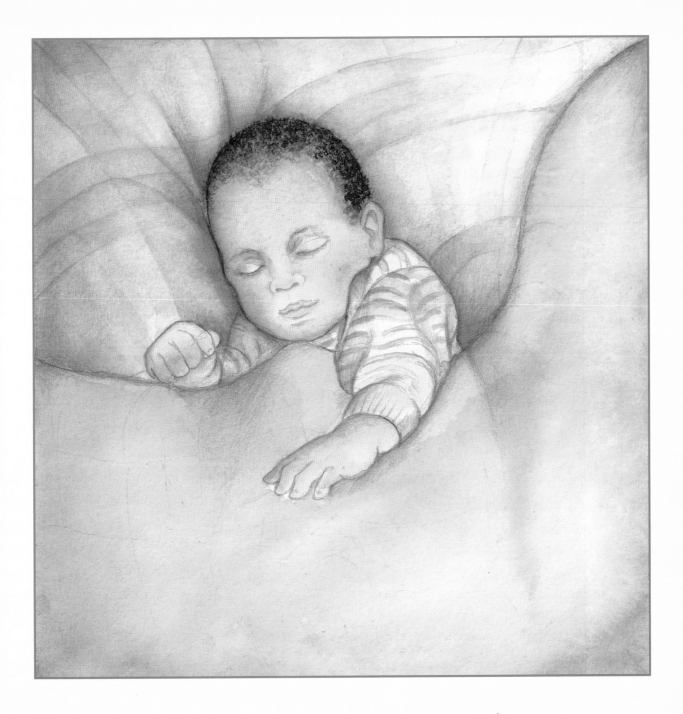

瑪花和森往裡面凝視，見到一個細小的嬰兒。

Martha and Sam peered inside and saw a tiny baby.

「她很細小，」森說道，「她能夠與我們一起玩嗎？」
「她或者會長大得很快。」瑪花說。

"She's very small," said Sam. "Will she be able to play with us?"
"Maybe she'll grow really quickly," said Martha.

她們觀察了整整兩個星期，但嬰兒並沒有快高長大。

They watched for two whole weeks,
but the baby didn't grow quickly.

當瑪花和森為嬰兒表演木偶戲時，她只顧吸吮她的姆指，並沒有留意看戲。

When Martha and　　　Sam put on a puppet show for the baby, she was too busy sucking her thumb to take any notice.

當她們為她演奏她們最喜愛的樂曲時，嬰兒却由頭睡到尾。

When they played her their favourite tune,
the baby slept right through it.

而當她們與小鳥交朋友時，嬰兒大聲叫喊把小鳥嚇走了！

And when they made friends with a bird,
the baby screamed so loudly she frightened it away!

「那嬰兒跟你不一樣，」森說道，「你應該把她遣回。」瑪花對森所說的話覺得很有趣，她便走去找媽媽。

"That baby is *not* just like you,"
said Sam. "You should send her back."
Martha felt funny when Sam said this and went to look for Mum.

媽媽正在為嬰兒忙。

「可以擁抱我嗎？」她問道。

「等一等，瑪花，」媽媽說。

Mum was busy.

"Can I have a cuddle?" she asked.

"Just a minute, Martha," said Mum.

「但我現在需要你啊！」瑪花嗚咽着説道，「你總是與她一起，而她跟我又不一樣，她不會做任何事。她甚麼時候才會是正式的妹妹呢？」

"But I need you *now*!" wailed Martha. "You're always with *her*. And she's *not* like me. She won't do *anything*. When is she going to be a proper sister?"

媽媽把嬰兒放下，並把
瑪花抱入臂彎。

Mum put the baby down and
scooped Martha into her arms.

「瑪花，你亦曾經像她一樣，看你已長得多大。」
「你是否愛我跟愛她一樣？」瑪花問道。
「一樣，」媽媽說，並將她緊緊抱着，「我仍然一樣愛你。」

"Martha, you were just like that once and look how you've grown."

"Did you love me as much as you love her?" asked Martha.

"Just as much," said Mum, holding her tight, "and I still do."

瑪花心裡覺得舒服些，便走回去跟森一起玩。

Martha felt better and went back to play with Sam.

媽媽說得對，是需要一段時間的，但嬰兒終於
開始成長了。

Mum was right. It took a while, but finally the baby began to grow.

她在她們的樂隊演奏。

She played in their band.

她看她們的木偶戲時大笑。

She laughed at their puppet show.

她更跟她們的小鳥交朋友。

She even made friends with their bird.

「你真是幸運，有一個小妹妹，」森說道。
「我知道，」瑪花說，「一個跟我一樣的妹妹。」

"You're ever so lucky to have a sister," said Sam.
"I know," said Martha. "A sister just like me."